The Unicorns of Blossom Wood

First published in the UK in 2016 by Scholastic Children's Books
An imprint of Scholastic Ltd
Euston House, 24 Eversholt Street
London, NW1 1DB, UK
Registered office: Westfield Road, Southam, Warwickshire, CV47 0RA
SCHOLASTIC and associated logos are trademarks and/or registered
trademarks of Scholastic Inc.

ISBN 978 1407 17123 4

A CIP catalogue record for this book is available from the British Library

Printed and bound by CPI Group (UK) Ltd, Croydon, CR0 4YY
Papers used by Scholastic Children's Books are made from wood
grown in sustainable forests.

10

This is a work of fiction. Names, characters, places, incidents and
dialogues are products of the author's imagination or are used
fictitiously. Any resemblance to actual people, living or dead,
events or locales is entirely coincidental.

www.scholastic.co.uk

Catherine Coe

Unicorn games
& quizzes
inside!

The Unicorns of Blossom Wood

❊ Festival Time ❊

■SCHOLASTIC

For the Bleippsons, whose amazing friendship is even better than magic xxx

Thanks to Dina von Lowenkraft for all your invaluable advice, and to Tom and Abi Holroyde, my readers down under!

Chapter 1

Let It Snow

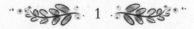

Pat, pat, pat. Patter, patter, patter.

Isabelle yawned and snuggled down further in her sleeping bag. The rain pattering on the tent had woken her up, but she wasn't ready to start the day yet. She was cosy and warm, lying in between her two cousins, Lei and Cora. They were still fast asleep – Lei snoring gently and Cora curled up in a ball so all Isabelle could see was her silky blonde hair. Isabelle wondered whether to wake them, but they looked so peaceful that she decided not to. Instead she pulled out her notebook and pen from under her pillow.

"Blossom Wood is the most beautiful place I've ever seen," she started to write. "It's so amazing it feels like a dream..."

She stopped suddenly. Maybe it *was* just a dream. Yesterday, Isabelle had thought that she and her cousins had been transported to a magical wood where they were no longer girls, but unicorns! But Isabelle always had very vivid dreams. Maybe this was just one of them? Her heart felt heavy – she'd be so disappointed if it wasn't real and they couldn't go back again. Now she couldn't wait any longer for Lei and Cora to wake up.

Isabelle gently shook their shoulders. Lei yelled, "Argh, what's happening?" while Cora uncurled and flashed open her blue eyes.

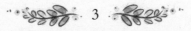

"Sorry!" said Isabelle, her heart pounding with worry now. "But I need to know something. Did I dream Blossom Wood, or was it real?"

Lei beamed, and her dark brown eyes twinkled. "It was real," she replied, nodding furiously.

Cora grinned too. "We turned into unicorns, we really did!"

Isabelle hugged both her cousins at once as relief flooded through her.

"Now, since you woke me up, I have a question for you," Lei said, leaping up from her sleeping bag. "When are we going back?"

Isabelle looked down at her purple checked pyjamas. "Um, we probably need to get dressed first!" she said. They'd got to Blossom Wood by stepping into some hoof prints in a nearby cove, but they

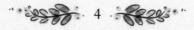

couldn't really leave the campsite in their sleeping gear... What would they tell their parents?

Lei pulled her long, dark hair into a ponytail, revealing the pink braids in her hair underneath. She grabbed her towel. "Come on then! Last one to the shower block has to clean up the tent!"

"But we're meant to be going on a hike today, remember," said Cora, the smile disappearing from her face. The three families were on holiday together – even though Cora lived in Australia, Isabelle in England and Lei in the USA, they always met up for a week or two during the summer holidays.

Lei unzipped the tent and looked out. "Yeah, but it's raining! Hopefully the hike will get cancelled."

Isabelle nodded, making her red

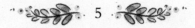

curls bounce about. She'd been looking forward to walking around the valleys here, but there was no way it'd be as good as another visit to Blossom Wood!

After they'd showered and dressed, they found their parents sitting on camping chairs under the awning of Lei's parents' tent. Isabelle's mum was handing out mugs, while Lei's dad set up their portable stove. Lei's older sister, Ying, lay on her back across the tarpaulin — headphones in, eyes shut, nodding her head to her music.

Cora's mum stared out at the rain, shaking her head. "Looks like the hike is off, girls. According to the forecast, it's going to rain all day."

Lei tried to look disappointed, but her insides bubbled with hope. Now they just had to figure out a reason to go down to

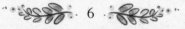

the cove with the hoof prints…

Lei's mum held up a guidebook. "There's a local café in here — it says they do the best cream cakes for miles, *and* they have an art gallery."

Lei's dad looked up from the stove. "Do they do tea and coffee too? I can't get this stove to work, no matter what I do!"

"Yes," his wife replied with a smile. "A selection of hot and cold drinks, according to this, plus pastries and doughnuts."

Cora's dad patted his stomach. "Sounds ace. Shall we have brekkie there then?"

The adults all nodded and got up from their chairs. "Get your umbrellas, girls," said Lei's mum. "It's about a ten-minute walk."

"Um … I'm not really hungry," said Isabelle.

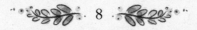

"Me neither," added Lei.

Isabelle's mum raised her eyebrows. "You don't want cakes for breakfast?"

They shook their heads. "I'm still stuffed from the barbie last night," said Cora, which was true, although cakes did sound good. Just not as good as becoming a unicorn!

"Can we stay here?" Lei asked. "Ying will keep an eye on us, won't you, Ying?"

Ying opened one eye, nodded, then closed it again.

"If you're sure," said Lei's dad. "I guess sitting in a café isn't very exciting. Just don't go too far from the campsite, OK?"

"We won't." Isabelle linked arms with Cora and Lei. It wasn't really a lie, because the hoof prints were close by. But of course Blossom Wood was a whole different world entirely!

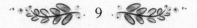

Five minutes later, Lei, Cora and Isabelle were running down the hill from their campsite towards a small blue lake. They weren't going far, just like they'd promised — down to a little cove at the side of the lake. And they knew no time would pass back here while they were away in Blossom Wood.

Their trainers squelched in the muddy ground and raindrops splattered on their faces, but they didn't mind. Soon they reached the sandy shore, and they sprinted into the cove — which was like a shallow cave in the hillside surrounded by pretty flowers.

"They're still there!" gasped Cora. She'd been worrying that the three sets of hoof prints in the rocky ground might have disappeared somehow. She jumped

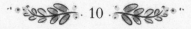

into the ones that matched her feet —
the biggest set — while Lei stepped into
the smallest prints and Isabelle into the
medium-sized ones.

Dazzling white light filled the cove,
making the girls close their eyes. "We're
going to Blossom Wood!" yelled Lei, as

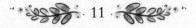

warmth shot through her feet and into her legs, body and arms.

"And we'll soon be unicorns!" added Isabelle, smiling as she felt hot tingles dance across her skin.

Cora trembled as the warm magic flooded through her. Before yesterday, she didn't even believe in magic, but now she was about to become a unicorn!

Sure enough, when the bright light faded and Cora opened her eyes, she saw shiny hooves where her feet used to be, and white unicorn legs instead of her normal two. When she looked up, she shrieked. Blossom Wood lay before her like last time they'd visited, but now there was one big difference: it was covered in sparkling snow.

The three cousins stared at the landscape from their position on the

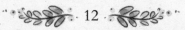

mountainside. "Wow," murmured
Isabelle. "I thought it looked beautiful
before. But the snow makes it seem even
more magical!"

Lei neighed in agreement. "Let's go
and find our woodland friends!" she said,

galloping off excitedly before her cousins could reply. Not that Isabelle and Cora minded – they wanted to meet up with the other animals too!

Chapter 2

The Mid-Winter Festival

Lei galloped down the rocky mountain path, the snow cold and crunchy beneath her hooves. Pink sparks flew as they touched the ground – matching the bright pink colour of her unicorn mane and tail. They knew that the sparks were magical, but Lei didn't know what type of magic she had yet. Cora did, though –

hers was healing magic, and last time they were here she had cured a badger's injured paw and a mouse's earache. Lei longed to find out what she could do, and hoped it would be just as special. *And anyway,* she told herself, *just being a unicorn is awesome enough – it's even better than riding my horse!*

"Wait for me!" yelled Isabelle, her red mane and tail flying out behind her as she cantered to keep up with her cousin. Lei was the shortest of the unicorns – the size of a small pony – and the slowest, but she'd got a head start on her cousins.

Behind them Cora trotted much more carefully – she worried that she might slip on the snowy ground, even though her hooves seemed steady. She was the biggest of the unicorns – sleek and

powerful like a racehorse – with a golden mane and tail. She began to feel more confident and quickened to a canter, enjoying the warm, magical feeling rushing through her legs, despite the cold of the snow beneath them. In the distance, she could see Lei and Isabelle near the bottom of the mountain. They were neighing in greeting at a smaller figure ahead of them. As Cora drew closer, she saw that it was a badger – but not just any badger. It was their friend Bobby!

As Cora drew closer, she noticed Bobby was beaming. "Hello, Cora," he said in his deep, gravelly voice. "I was just telling Isabelle and Lei that it's our mid-winter festival here today!"

"Hi, Bobby," she replied with a nicker. Even after meeting him yesterday, she

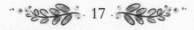

couldn't quite believe she was speaking to a talking badger. It was crazy, really – but a good kind of crazy!

Bobby wrapped his scarf tighter around his neck. "You must come and join in. We've been wondering when you'd come back to see us. I promise you that it's one of the most magical days we have in Blossom Wood!"

"We'd love to!" said Lei, kicking up
her front hooves playfully. She guessed
that days and seasons must be very
different in Blossom Wood compared to
home – it sounded like lots of time had
passed here since their first visit!

They let Bobby take the lead as they
trotted through the stunning snow-
covered wood. "That's Badger Falls,
where I live," he explained, pointing
to the entrance holes of badger setts
near a frozen waterfall. "And over
there is the Oval of Oaks. Remember
Mo, the mouse whose earache you
cured, Cora? He lives there, with his
wife, May."

Bobby continued to point places out
along the way, and Isabelle tried to
remember everything as best she could.
There was the Brown Desert, where the

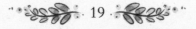

deer had run away from them because they hadn't believed in unicorns. Luckily they did now, thanks to Bobby. And of course the desert wasn't brown today, because it, like everything else, was blanketed in shining white snowflakes. But the snow here seemed different to the snow she'd seen at home – brighter and more sparkly. And she didn't feel cold at all. Maybe it was her unicorn magic!

Cora didn't say a word as they walked along. She simply stared in amazement at the thick snow lining the trees and the ground around her – she'd never seen snow before, because it didn't get cold enough to snow in Australia. The seasons had to be different here in Blossom Wood – because it was summer back at the Hilltop Hideaway campsite! And

last time they'd been here it hadn't been winter, but spring!

Lei didn't get snow where she lived either – she was from San Francisco – and all she could think about was whether there'd be time to build a snowman, which was something she'd

dreamt of ever since she saw the *Snowman* movie. She began to wonder how she'd make one as a unicorn. With her hooves? Could she push snow into a ball with her nose?

"Here we are!" said Bobby. He pointed ahead, at snow-covered willow trees, and below them all sorts of different creatures scampered about.

Isabelle giggled at the sight of deer in bobble hats and squirrels wearing gloves. She could even see bees with tiny earmuffs and blackbirds wearing snow boots! There were wooden stalls set out below the trees, filled with drinks and snacks and winter gifts.

As they got closer, the animals around the stalls waved at the unicorns, shouting "Hello!" and "Welcome back!" and "It's so good to see you!"

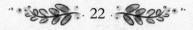

It's totally different from when we first came here, thought Cora, remembering that the woodlanders were all scared of the unicorns at first, because they didn't believe they existed. Luckily Bobby had helped to change their minds, and now everyone was super friendly.

The cousins neighed greetings and flicked their ears as Bobby led them further. Lei gasped as they stepped through the line of glistening willow trees. There beyond them was the most magical sight of all – a gleaming lake, frozen with ice, with hundreds of little creatures skating across its surface.

"Hi, there!" squeaked a squirrel gliding along the edge in front of them.

"G'day, Loulou!" Cora replied, recognizing the animal from their last visit here.

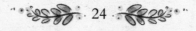

"Are you coming ice skating?" Loulou asked with a grin.

Cora shook her head quickly. "Oh no, I don't think so – the ice might not be strong enough for unicorns. And I'm not sure I can swim!" Of course Cora could swim as a girl – she swam in the Australian sea every weekend in the summer – and she knew horses could

swim. But she had no idea how to do it as a unicorn!

A caterpillar in a knitted hat popped up beside Lei. He held out an acorn filled with steaming liquid. "Would you like some walnut-spiced tea?" he asked.

Lei sniffed. It smelt so good – sweet and spicy and nutty. "Yes, please!" He set it down and she lowered her head and slurped it in one go. It tasted just as good as it smelt. "Thank you, Wilf!" she said to the caterpillar.

"You must try my baked apple tarts," said a deer, walking over to Isabelle.

"Hi, Sara," Isabelle replied, glad to see that Sara wasn't running away like the first time she'd met her. The deer was beaming, and holding out a large golden-brown tart in her teeth.

"Please take this one for you and Cora and Lei," Sara insisted in her smooth voice. "I have lots more for everyone. I've been baking for days!"

"That's really kind, thank you." Isabelle whinnied to show her thanks, then bent down and took a big bite of the tart. "Mmmmmm…" she said, savouring the delicious rich and fruity mouthful. She passed the tart to Cora, who took a polite little bite, but quickly followed it with a much bigger one!

Bobby suddenly clapped his paws and nodded at the iced-over Willow Lake. "The butterflies' winter dance is about to start!" The unicorns looked over. No one was skating on the lake any more – instead, hundreds of light pink butterflies were flying above it, moving into position for their performance.

They look like daytime fireworks, thought Isabelle as she watched them fluttering up into the cloudy white sky.

Lei heard a squeaky noise behind her, and tore her gaze from the butterflies to find out what it was.

"Help! Quick!" came a high little voice.

Lei spotted a rabbit running towards them. "What's wrong?" she asked.

"It's my sister! She's stuck in the mountains!" the bunny cried.

Chapter 3

Unicorns to the Rescue

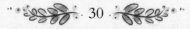

"Whatever do you mean, Billy?" asked Bobby, his black eyebrows knitted with concern.

Billy pointed to Echo Mountains, far in the distance. "We were looking for fossils for our festival stall, but we went off in different directions, and then I couldn't find Lizzie. I looked for AGES!"

Cora wanted to give the rabbit a hug, he looked so upset. But being a unicorn, that wasn't so easy. Instead, she bent her head down gently so it was level with his. "It's OK, Billy. It's not your fault. Are you sure she didn't come back without you?"

Billy shook his head. "No – I've checked here already. And we promised that we'd meet at the cave entrance if we got split up. But I went there, and she never came!"

Lei moved her head down to Billy now, meeting his little black eyes with her brown ones. "Don't worry, Billy," she told the rabbit. He looked like he might burst into tears at any moment. "We'll find her."

Bobby put an arm around the young bunny. "You did the right thing coming

to get help. You stay here with me while
the unicorns go and search for Lizzie.
You'd better go and tell your mum too.
But tell her not to worry. The unicorns
will sort all this out for us. Thank

treetops that they're here just at the right time!"

Cora looked at her cousins. She hoped more than anything that they could find Lizzie, but what if they couldn't? It seemed the animals of Blossom Wood were relying on them!

Impatient to start looking, Lei stamped the ground with her foot, and pink sparks flew up like glitter around it. "Come on," she said to her cousins. "Let's go!"

Cora nodded, and Isabelle took a last look at the gorgeous butterfly display above the lake. The white clouds looked thicker now, as if it might snow again at any moment. Isabelle wished she could stay to see the butterflies' dance, but finding Lizzie was much more important. "We'll be back soon," she

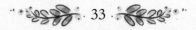

reassured Bobby, and the three unicorns rushed off, making deep hoof prints in the snow.

"Thank you!" they heard Billy call after them in his high-pitched bunny voice.

As they galloped along, the snow crunching beneath their hooves, Cora spoke. "Do you really think we'll be able to find Lizzie?" She didn't feel very confident – they'd never even been inside the caves in Echo Mountains before.

"Of course we will!" said Lei, tossing her mane and staring at her cousin. "How can you even doubt it?"

Cora didn't reply, and instead turned her head away from Lei.

Lei immediately felt bad for speaking so angrily. Cora was the opposite of her in some ways – sensible and not very

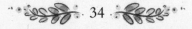

confident — and Lei knew she was often too headstrong. "I'm sorry," she told Cora. "I'm just determined to get poor Lizzie out."

"No, you're right," Cora realized, looking back at Lei. "We've got to do everything we can to find her."

"Oh, look!" As she galloped, Isabelle tipped her head skywards. "It's snowing!"

Lei looked up and gasped. She was speechless, which was  VERY unlike Lei. She'd thought seeing the snow on the trees and ground was amazing, but watching it fall in fluffy flakes was even better! She batted her

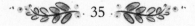

eyelashes as snowflakes fell on them. It was the most incredible feeling.

"I love snow," said Isabelle. "It always looks so magical and sparkly, and here it's even better!" They were nearing the mountains now, and could see the entrance to the caves at the end of a wide path dotted with bunny pawprints.

"Do you think our magic will help us find Lizzie?" Cora wondered out loud. She wasn't sure her healing magic would help, but maybe Isabelle's or Lei's magic would. The only problem was that they didn't even know what their magic was yet!

"It has to!" said Lei, finding her voice. She felt more determined than ever. "We promised Billy!"

Lei reached the cave entrance first,

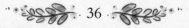

and ducked inside without even thinking about it.

"What's it like in there?" asked Cora, worrying that it would be pitch-black.

"Pretty dark," Lei admitted. Her voice

sounded echoey inside the mountains. "But it's fine. My eyes are adjusting really fast!"

Cora stopped outside and peered in. It was so black she couldn't see Lei at all – not even her pink tail or mane!

"I'll go next," Isabelle offered, trotting happily past Cora and into the cave.

Cora heard Lei gasp. "That's awesome!"

"Oh, oh, oh!" Isabelle murmured in reply.

Cora wondered what was going on. Her cousins didn't sound worried at all. They sounded excited!

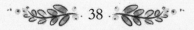

Chapter 4

Into Echo Mountains

"Come in here, Cora, quick!" yelled Lei.

This time, when Cora peered inside, she could see Isabelle – and her whole body was surrounded by white light! Cora trotted inside, closer to her cousins.

"Do it again!" Lei told Isabelle.

Isabelle gave a neigh, and then pranced

in place, making red sparks shoot off her hooves. They rose to her legs and her body, then to her head and her horn. The white light around Isabelle grew brighter and brighter and brighter.

"It's your magic!" Cora realized. "You can make light!"

Isabelle spun around. "I know! Crazy, huh?" She looked like the most incredible unicorn-shaped lantern, and the light she gave off was so strong they could see all around the dark cave.

Lei nudged Cora. "You don't have to be afraid of the dark now!" she told her.

Cora turned to her cousin. "I'm not afraid!" she said.

"I'm only joking," Lei said with a smile. "Anyway, I agree – it's much nicer in here now that we have glow-in-the-dark Isabelle!"

Isabelle whinnied. "I like that name! Right, now we can see, let's find Lizzie!"

With Isabelle's light guiding the way, they trotted through the cave. Luckily, they found tunnels that weren't too

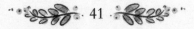

low or narrow, and only Cora, the tallest of the three, had to duck her head sometimes to avoid a low-hanging stalactite. Stalagmites grew from the floor too — like thick, upside-down icicles. Except...

"They're all different colours!" Lei realized, pointing her head towards a group of turquoise ones nearby.

"What do you mean?" Isabelle asked. She'd never seen any because she hadn't been in a cave before.

"They're usually creamy-coloured," Cora explained. "But these are all the colours of the rainbow!"

The unicorns stopped and stared at the beautiful pointy things for a moment, then Lei gave a loud neigh. "Let's go — we've got to find Lizzie!"

Cora and Isabelle nodded as Lei

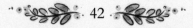

charged through the caves. Being the smallest unicorn, it was easy for Lei to twist and turn along the tunnels.

But Isabelle wasn't far behind, lighting up the way – the magic sparks flew up through her hooves, body and horn to create the light. The magic made her hot, but not horribly so – just as if she were surrounded by the heat of a warm log fire.

At the back, Cora made sure she stayed close to Isabelle, while looking left and right for any sign of Billy's sister.

"Lizzie!" Lei called, then "LIZZIE!" even louder. The unicorns listened, but they heard no reply except the echoes of their own voices. They kept going, deeper and deeper and deeper into the caves. The air grew even colder, and as Lei puffed and panted she could

see her breath rising up like mist.

They cantered into a large cavern, full to bursting with stunning stalactites that hung from the ceiling. *I'm going to write about this when I get home*, thought Isabelle. *It looks like something from Narnia!* A sound broke into her thoughts. What was it? Isabelle listened more carefully, stopping for a moment at the edge of the cavern.

"Hello," came a quiet, squeaky voice. "Hello?"

"Wait!" Isabelle yelled to Lei, who had galloped almost out of sight. Lei skipped to a stop and turned around.

Behind Isabelle, Cora had stopped too. "What's up?" Cora asked her cousin.

"Listen," Isabelle said, her voice a low hush.

"Is anyone there?"

The squeak was coming from the other side of the cavern. The unicorns trotted carefully between the stalagmites to get closer. As they neared, the voice got louder, and Isabelle spotted what she thought looked like a furry grey body.

"Lizzie?" Isabelle asked gently. On top of the body, a cute little rabbit's head twisted around, ears and whiskers twitching. But the bunny didn't move much – it looked like her tail was trapped under a rock!

"I'm stuck!" Lizzie squeaked

"Don't worry," said Lei. "We've come to rescue you."

Cora trotted closer. "Are you all right?" she asked Lizzie, thinking of how long she must have been down in the caves by herself. "It's so dark down here." *Well, it was before Isabelle came along!* Cora thought.

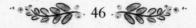

"Oh, yes, I'm fine!" Lizzie replied with a wave of her paw. "I'm used to being in the dark – our burrow is pitch-black too. But I was getting a bit bored, and guessed little Billy would be panicking about me."

Isabelle laughed. At least Lizzie hadn't been scared and lonely down here. "Billy

was so worried about you," she told the rabbit. "He said he couldn't find you anywhere!"

"It was my fault," Lizzie admitted, sounding a bit embarrassed. "I ran off, because I knew there were even better fossils here, and I wanted to get the best one for our stall. Then as I eased out a shiny fossil from the cave wall, I accidentally pulled this rock down on to my tail!"

Lei was already pushing her head at the large brown rock that had pinned Lizzie's tail to the ground. She gritted her teeth. "It won't move!" she panted.

"Let me help," said Cora, moving towards the rock. Isabelle trotted closer to provide as much light as she could.

Cora stood next to Lei, their muzzles resting on the rock. "One, two, three,

and push!" said Lei. Cora pushed as hard as she could ... and felt the rock moving. Was it enough?

"I'm free!" yelped Lizzie, jumping around and away from the rock. The bunny grinned, then frowned and rubbed her tail with a paw.

"Does it hurt?" Cora asked.

Lizzie rubbed at it again but put on a brave face. "It's fine, really. It's only a little bit sore..."

"But I can help," said Cora. "In case it is injured. Wait one minute..."

Cora pranced in place, and golden sparks shot up from her hooves. She kept trotting on the spot, and soon the sparks rose from her legs to her body to her head and her horn. With them, heat spread through Cora like a wave, and she felt tingly with magic. She leant down

her head and touched Lizzie's tail
with her horn.

Lizzie kept extremely still – all except
her face, where a great big smile was
appearing. "It feels as good as new,"

she said with a little shake of her tail. "Thank you! You unicorns are amazing!"

Cora, Lei and Isabelle all nickered in reply – a low, rumbling sound to show how happy they were.

"Now, should we get outta here?" said Lei. "I don't know about you, but I want to go back and check out the mid–winter festival!"

Isabelle nodded and looked around. "Just one question. How *do* we get out of here?"

Chapter 5
The Way Out

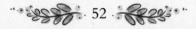

Lei stomped a front hoof on the ground, sending sparks flying, tossed her pink mane and frowned hard.

"What's the matter?" Isabelle asked her cousin.

"I didn't leave a trail!" Lei stamped a hoof again, feeling angry at herself.

"A trail?" squeaked Lizzie.

"Yes, a trail to get out of here! Everyone knows that's what you do so you don't get lost."

Cora nodded, understanding what Lei meant. She remembered this happening in at least three different books she'd read. If you left a trail then you could find your way back again easily by following it! But they hadn't done that.

"That's OK," said Lizzie with a smile. "I know how to get out! Follow me!"

"See, no need to worry," Isabelle told Lei, and her frown disappeared.

Isabelle stamped her hooves on the ground and sparkles flew as her magical light shimmered even brighter. They trotted behind Lizzie to the other side of the cavern.

But Lei's frown soon came back again when Lizzie scampered through a narrow

tunnel much, MUCH too small for the unicorns to squeeze into.

Soon, despite Isabelle's light, Lizzie had disappeared completely through the winding tunnel.

"Wait!" Lei shouted, poking her head into the small tunnel. "Lizzie!"

Lizzie spun around and ran backwards. "Oh, chestnuts!" she said, realizing what had stopped the unicorns. "But this is the only way I know out of here..."

Isabelle looked around. "Maybe there's another way?" She began trotting around the edge of the cavern, looking into each hole in case it was a tunnel out. "Can anyone remember how we came in?"

Cora hung her head. "No, sorry. I was too busy looking for Lizzie."

Lei cantered to the far side of the cavern. "Let's try down here!"

"But what if it's the wrong way?" replied Cora, feeling hot with panic. "What if we get even more lost?"

"She's right," said Isabelle. "It's too risky." An idea popped into her head. "Maybe we could use unicorn magic to make ourselves smaller?"

Lei neighed. "Maybe that's my magic!" She began prancing in place, sending pink sparks shooting up around her, trotting so quickly that the sparks soon moved over her legs and body, and to her head and neck. They fizzed and tingled her skin, and the warmth around her felt like Californian sunshine. When the sparks reached her horn, she waited. But nothing happened. She tried touching her horn to Isabelle, but nothing happened then either.

"Argh!" Lei yelled, stamping all of her hooves. "I wish I knew what my magic was!"

Lizzie scampered over to Lei and looked up into her big brown eyes. "Please don't be angry," she said to the unicorn. "I've got an idea. I'll run out

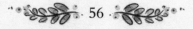

56

to get help – someone else will know how to get out of here down the bigger tunnels. And I'll be back as quick as I can, promise!"

Cora nodded. "That sounds like a good plan."

Lizzie smiled. "Don't worry, I'll have you out of here soon!"

As the rabbit ran off, Lei pressed her ears back in frustration. "But we can't just wait here doing nothing!" She paced backwards and forwards, stamping the rocky ground even more.

More pink sparks flew up, and Isabelle started to wonder if their sparks and magic might ever run out. If so, Lei was in danger of losing hers!

"I guess we could have a little look around," Cora suggested, wanting to make her cousin feel better.

Isabelle put her ears forward calmly. "Yes, and we don't have to go far. We could leave a trail back to the cavern this time, and then we won't get any more lost."

Lei looked up, her eyes brighter now. "We can use the pebbles lying near the edges of the walls." She began kicking little stones towards one opening. "I'll look down here!"

"I'll go with you," said Isabelle. "So you can see!"

But Lei shook her pink mane. "It's OK, I don't mind the dark. And I promise I won't go far."

"If you're sure? I'll try this way, then," Isabelle said, trotting to a hole at the other end of the cavern. "Cora, do you want to come with me?"

Cora did, really, but she was thinking about Lizzie. What if she returned to the cavern with help and they'd all disappeared! "I'll stay here. In case Lizzie comes back."

"But will you be OK in the dark?" Isabelle asked, widening her green eyes in concern.

"I'll be fine," Cora replied bravely. As Isabelle trotted away and the light faded, Cora wished she had her music

player with her. Because then she wouldn't feel by herself at all, but in the same room as her favourite bands and singers. Although Cora wondered whether her earbuds would fit in her unicorn ears...

It didn't matter, though, because she wasn't alone for long.

"Cora!" came a neighing voice just a few minutes later. "I've found someone..."

Isabelle's glossy white head and bright red mane appeared back in the cavern. The light around her also lit up a smaller creature by her side – the orangey-red figure of a fox!

Cora trotted closer to them, pleased to have Isabelle's magic light back. "Hello," she said with a neigh. "Can you help us get out of here?"

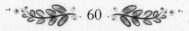

The fox rolled his eyes. "I could ...
but tell me why I *should*!"

"He's a bit grumpy," Isabelle whispered
in Cora's ear. "But I think we can win
him over."

Cora looked at the fox. His frowning
face didn't seem very win-over-able.

"What's going on?" shouted Lei, her

voice echoing from the tunnel. "I heard voices. Have you found a way out?"

Cora chewed her lip. "Kind of."

Lei's white head and pink mane appeared in the dark hole she'd disappeared down. She grinned and trotted towards them through the stalagmites. "Hello, Mr Fox. Boy, do we need your help!"

The fox bared his teeth. "First you call me Mr Fox. Then you say I'm just a 'boy'. How rude! And you unicorns are so demanding. It's your silly fault for getting lost in the first place!"

"I didn't mean 'boy' in that way!" Lei argued. "I—"

Isabelle interrupted before the fox got even angrier. "It's true that it's our fault," she said gently. "But maybe we could do something in return for you…"

The fox snorted. "I don't need anything from you! You wander into these caves, which you know nothing about, then disturb me from my nap. I don't see why I should help!"

He spun around and began to stride away, and the three cousins glanced at each other. Now what?

Lei thought quickly. How could they persuade the fox to help them? He'd said that they didn't know anything about the caves, which was sort of true, but...

"I know about stalactites!" Lei blurted out.

The fox stopped mid-walk, and swung back around again. "What do you mean?"

Lei bent her head down to the fox's level. "You said we didn't know anything about the caves, but we do! I know that

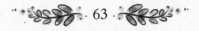

stalactites are made by water dripping down into the cave through cracks in the ceiling."

For the first time, the fox gave a hint of a smile. "Very good. But what about stalag*mites*? How are they made? If you

can tell me that, *then* I'll help you out of the cave." The fox looked at her slyly, as if he was sure she wouldn't know the answer.

Cora and Isabelle looked at their cousin. Did Lei know? Whether they were stuck in this cave or not depended on it!

Chapter 6

A Winter Wonderland

Lei nodded at a nearby stalagmite – a bright blue one. Above it, another blue one dripped water directly on its point. "That's easy! The water drips down from the stalactite to make stalagmites below. Look – those two have even closed together!" Lei flicked her pink tail at a shiny purple column – where a stalactite

and stalagmite had grown so tall they'd joined together.

The fox was shaking his orange head. "Well, I never. Not many people know that. You unicorns aren't just full of pretty magic – you're clever too!" He beckoned down the tunnel in front of him. "Come on then. This way!"

The unicorns trotted after him quickly. "Well done, Lei," Cora whispered.

Lei smiled. "I'm just glad he didn't ask me why the stalactites and stalagmites are different colours in Blossom Wood. I have no clue about that!"

The fox shot down the tunnels and the unicorns galloped after him. He was shorter than they were, of course, but he took a large enough route for them to get through the caves easily. He seemed to know exactly where he was going, but then, if he lived here, it wasn't surprising, thought Cora. She was just glad Isabelle had found him!

After only a few minutes, Isabelle saw a white circle in the distance –

different from the light that shone around her. "The way out!" she said to her cousins. Now she didn't need to create magic to make light any more, her red sparks stayed around her hooves.

All three unicorns gasped as they caught up to the fox, who had come to a stop beside the hole to the outside. There must have been a snowstorm while they were inside the caves, because the snow lay in big drifts now – like a thick duvet across the ground.

"It's a real winter wonderland!" said Isabelle. She stepped out into the snowflakes and pranced in place. Lei quickly followed, but Cora held back.

"Thank you for helping us, Mr Fox," she said.

He looked up at her and smiled

properly now. "Please, call me Freddy. And I might be grumpy, but I keep my promises. Now, try not to get lost on your way to the mid-winter festival!"

Cora frowned. "You're not coming too?"

"Oh no – hundreds of creatures being jolly is my worst nightmare. I'm staying right here."

"OK, then," Cora replied. She decided not to try to persuade Freddy to come. He didn't sound like he'd be much fun at a party. She bobbed her head, then galloped off, but the thick snow stopped her from going very fast.

"Freddy's not coming," she said as she caught up to her cousins. They hadn't got very far either. Since she was the biggest and most powerful of the unicorns, Cora moved to the front to push a path through the snow drifts. It was fun, like wading through mud, but hard work!

"Freddy?" Lei asked, confused.

Cora neighed. "The fox!"

Isabelle giggled. "He told you his name? Maybe he's not as grumpy as we thought."

"Oh yes he is." Cora laughed. "He

said the festival would be his worst nightmare!"

"Speaking of the festival — there it is!" Lei nodded her head towards Willow Lake, just ahead of them.

Bobby raised his arms up and beamed when he saw the unicorns. "You're back! Thank treetops! We were just about to send out a search party to find you in the caves."

Lizzie ran over and hugged one of Isabelle's front legs. Then she moved on to Lei, and then Cora. "You're out OK! I was just about to come back with help. What happened?"

"We found a fox, and he helped us out!" Lei explained.

Bobby frowned. "Freddy? But he never helps anyone. He's the grumpiest of all the woodlanders by far."

"We know!" said all three unicorns together.

"Luckily Lei impressed him with her cave knowledge," said Isabelle. "But he still refused to come to the mid-winter festival. Have we missed much?"

Loulou scampered towards her. "Nothing!" the squirrel squeaked. "There was such a blizzard while you were in

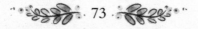

the caves that we had to put the party on hold."

"But now the snow has almost stopped, we can start again," added Bobby in his gravelly voice.

The pale pink butterflies were gathering in the sky above Willow Lake once more. A band of ducks started up, playing acorn drums and tulip trumpets, and the butterflies began to dance.

"They're so pretty!" said Isabelle, her ears flicking with happiness. The butterflies flew in circles, then figures of eight, then like waves across the sky. It was so beautiful it made her insides feel all warm and gooey.

As the butterflies' performance ended and the duck band changed their music to a swinging tune, a little brown bird buzzed over.

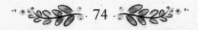

"Hi, I'm Winnie," she said in a sing-song voice. "It's fan-doobly-tastic to meet you! Would you like some honey drizzle cake?"

"That sounds yummy!" Lei replied as her stomach roared. She suddenly realized they'd missed breakfast. The only thing she'd eaten all day was a bite of Sara's apple tart.

Winnie led the unicorns to her stall on the edge of Willow Lake. It was piled high with glistening honey cakes which made Cora's mouth water immediately.

"Here, take two each," said Winnie. "I heard about your brave rescue mission – you deserve them!"

"Thank you," Cora said, before eating half a cake in one bite. The sweet honey coated her mouth in oozy deliciousness,

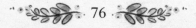

and the cake was so soft it melted on her tongue.

"This is the best cake I've ever tasted!" Cora told Winnie, meaning every word.

Winnie beamed from ear to ear. "I can give you the recipe if you'd like?"

Cora nickered. "Oh, yes, please."

While Winnie told Cora the honey cake recipe, Lei bit into her cake and trotted over to the fossil stall. Lizzie and Billy were standing behind it, grinning.

"Oh, Lei, thank you from the very bottom of my tail for rescuing Lizzie," Billy squeaked. He leapt across the fossil-covered stall and landed on Lei's neck to give her a hug.

"Billy, don't jump on the unicorn!" said Lizzie, shaking her fluffy head.

Lei laughed. "It's OK," she said. "He's as light as a feather!"

Billy hugged her tighter, while Lizzie held something out in her paws. Lei trotted closer to take a look.

"Please have this — it's the fossil I found when I got stuck. The best one. You deserve to have it."

Lei looked at the bunny rabbit. "Are you sure?" she said slowly. The fossil was the prettiest stone she'd even seen – covered in green and blue shimmering lines. And the shape of it even looked a bit like a unicorn head!

"I insist," Lizzie replied. "I think it looks like a unicorn, don't you?"

Lei smiled at the rabbit. "Thank you. I will treasure it for ever!" She plucked it up and tucked it into the side of her mouth, where she could keep it safely.

Nearby, Isabelle was sipping a chestnut cup of elderflower tea, while watching the duck band with Bobby. They played "What a Wonderful Wood" and "I'm a Woodlander" and "Mid-Winter Sunset" and one of them, a duck called Monty, sang along at the front. Many creatures danced, but after all the galloping she'd done that day, Isabelle was happy just to watch.

"It's time for the snowman competition!" Bobby announced when the duck band finished their last tune. "Who's joining in?"

"Shall we, shall we?" said Lei, trotting over and neighing with excitement.

Cora cantered over too. "I've never built a snowman…"

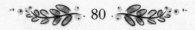

Isabelle nodded. "Then we've got to change that right now!"

The unicorns got to work. Isabelle showed Cora and Lei how to roll the snow carefully along the ground with their hooves, making balls that grew bigger and bigger and bigger.

It was only when Isabelle was using her nose to nudge the snowman head up on to the body that she noticed something. "Wow! These snowflakes have eight sides, not six!"

"But that's impossible," said Lei.

Cora whinnied. "Nothing's impossible in Blossom Wood!"

"I guess you're right," Lei decided, looking at a snowflake, her eyes wide.

When they'd finished, Bobby came around to judge the competition. "Good effort," he told the unicorns. "But I think I'm going to have to make Billy and Lizzie's the winner..."

Lei, Cora and Isabelle turned to look at the rabbits' snowman and gasped. They'd made a snow unicorn, with the words "Unicorns are the best!" written on its side.

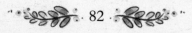

"Ha – that's definitely the winner!" said Isabelle, kicking up her hooves in delight.

Bobby gave the rabbits their prize – a beautiful ice sculpture of the Moon Chestnut tree, which was the oldest and most magical tree in the forest. "Congratulations!" Then he added, "It's getting late. The festival will finish soon."

Isabelle looked up. They'd been so busy building their snowman that she hadn't noticed it was growing dark.

"We should go," said Cora, feeling exhausted all of a sudden.

Lei neighed. Though she didn't like to admit it, she was beat now too. "Thank you, Bobby, and all of the woodlanders, for an amazing day. See you again soon?"

"Oh, I do hope so, dear unicorns,"

said Bobby, nodding seriously. "Blossom Wood isn't the same without you! I cannot thank you enough for what you did today."

Cora, Isabelle and Lei said goodbye to all their woodland friends before making their way back to the special hoof prints in Echo Mountains that would take them home. It was getting cooler now it was dusk, and Cora was looking forward to the warmth of her sleeping bag. Since time stopped while they were away, they'd just have to tell Ying they needed a morning nap!

"What a magical day," she whispered as they trotted towards the hoof prints. "It's shame we don't have anything to remind us of it."

Lei giggled then. "But we do!" she cried, moving the fossil she'd been

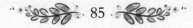

keeping safe in her mouth between her lips for the others to see. Cora and Isabelle gasped at the beautiful unicorn-like fossil.

"Then it's been perfect!" Isabelle decided as she stepped into the hoof prints and heat tingled in her hooves, legs and body.

As bright white light flashed all around and they closed their eyes, her cousins nodded. No one could argue with that.

Did You Know?

❀ In winter-time, waterfalls really do
   sometimes freeze over, just as Badger
   Falls has in the story. They look really
   pretty!

❀ Cora was right not to try to ice skate
   on Willow Lake – even though frozen
   lakes and ponds can look fun to skate
   on, sometimes the ice isn't as strong as
   it looks, and it can be very dangerous.

❀ Just as Lei says, stalactites grow in
   caves when water drips down from
   above. The longest stalactite in the
   world is in a cave in Lebanon, and is
   over eight metres long. That's about
   the height of a two-storey house!

❀ Because water drips down from a
   stalactite to create the stalagmite below,
   if they grow large enough they come

together to create a column. The tallest stalagmite is in China, and stretches to seventy metres. That's higher than Tower Bridge in London!

Word Search

Can you find five animals that live in Blossom Wood in this word search?

L	F	O	Y	H	S	W	C	F	I
P	B	A	D	G	E	R	N	K	J
D	I	U	A	H	F	S	Z	P	O
H	A	E	T	C	X	Q	I	W	M
K	Q	Y	W	T	D	U	R	H	F
L	D	X	D	B	E	I	Z	D	C
N	R	I	E	W	V	R	J	A	T
M	O	L	E	Q	X	R	F	I	H
A	T	C	R	B	S	E	V	L	W
Z	J	F	H	Q	G	L	O	T	Y

❀ Badger ❀ Butterfly ❀ Deer

❀ Mole ❀ Squirrel

Spot The Difference

Can you spot five things that are different in these pictures?

Unicorns To The Rescue!

Can you help Cora, Lei and Isabelle find Lizzie who is trapped in the cave?

Start

Finish

Isabelle Fact File

In this story, Isabelle discovers her light magic. Here are some other fun facts about Isabelle.

Name: Isabelle Sutton

Age: 9

Family: Lives with her mum but sees her dad at weekends (no brothers or sisters)

Home town: Norwich, Norfolk, UK

Pets: None – but she has made friends with many of the birds living in her garden!

Favourite drink: Hot chocolate

Favourite word: Wow

Favourite book: *The Lion, the Witch and the Wardrobe* by C. S. Lewis

Likes: Acting, writing, drawing and making up games to play

Dislikes: Sitting still for too long

Meet

The Owls of Blossom Wood

in these magical books

Turn over for a sneak peek of another
The Unicorns of Blossom Wood adventure!

Catherine Coe

Unicorn games
& quizzes
inside!

The
Unicorns of
Blossom Wood
Believe in Magic

Chapter 2

Blossom Wood

After a few seconds, the bright light began to fade. Lei was the first to open her eyes, and the sight was so shocking, she found she couldn't speak for a moment. She stood on a mountain, with a beautiful woodland landscape stretching out below her – filled with blossoming trees in every direction. She could see a

glimmering lake in the distance, edged by willow trees, and a winding river rushing towards it. Closer by was a tree much taller than the rest, with a curved trunk which Lei thought looked like a crescent moon. The air buzzed with the sound of animals and birds chirping and whistling as they went about their daily business.

"Where ARE we?" Lei asked, looking all around. That was when she noticed something was different. VERY different. Where her feet used to be, there were shiny hooves. And her legs had changed too — they looked like the furry white legs of a horse!

She stumbled backwards — on her hind legs — and saw the backs of two white horses beside her. "C-Cora, Isabelle, is that y-you?!" she stammered.

The two white horses turned around and nodded, their eyes dazzled with shock. But by the look of the horns coming out of her cousins' heads, they weren't horses at all – they were unicorns!

Isabelle, who had a curly, bright red mane and tail, just like her hair, began trotting around. "This is AMAZING!" she cried. "We're unicorns!"

But Cora was shaking her head frantically, making her golden mane swoosh from side to side. "No, no, no – I must be imagining this! It must be the jet lag. It can't be real!"

Lei noticed a shallow pool of water behind them, in the shadows of the mountainside, and had an idea. She nudged Cora towards it. "Look at your reflection. It IS real!"

Cora slowly trotted over to the pool, and Isabelle joined her. The shadows seemed to brighten as the three of them bent their heads to look at the water.

"Magic," Isabelle whispered as three long unicorn heads stared back at them from the pool...

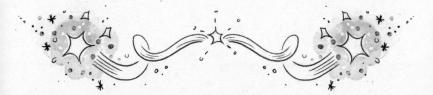

Would you like more animal
fun and facts?

Fancy flying across the treetops in
a magical Blossom Wood game?

Want sneak peeks of other
books in the series?

Then check out the
Blossom Wood website at:

blossomwoodbooks.com

The Unicorns of Blossom Wood